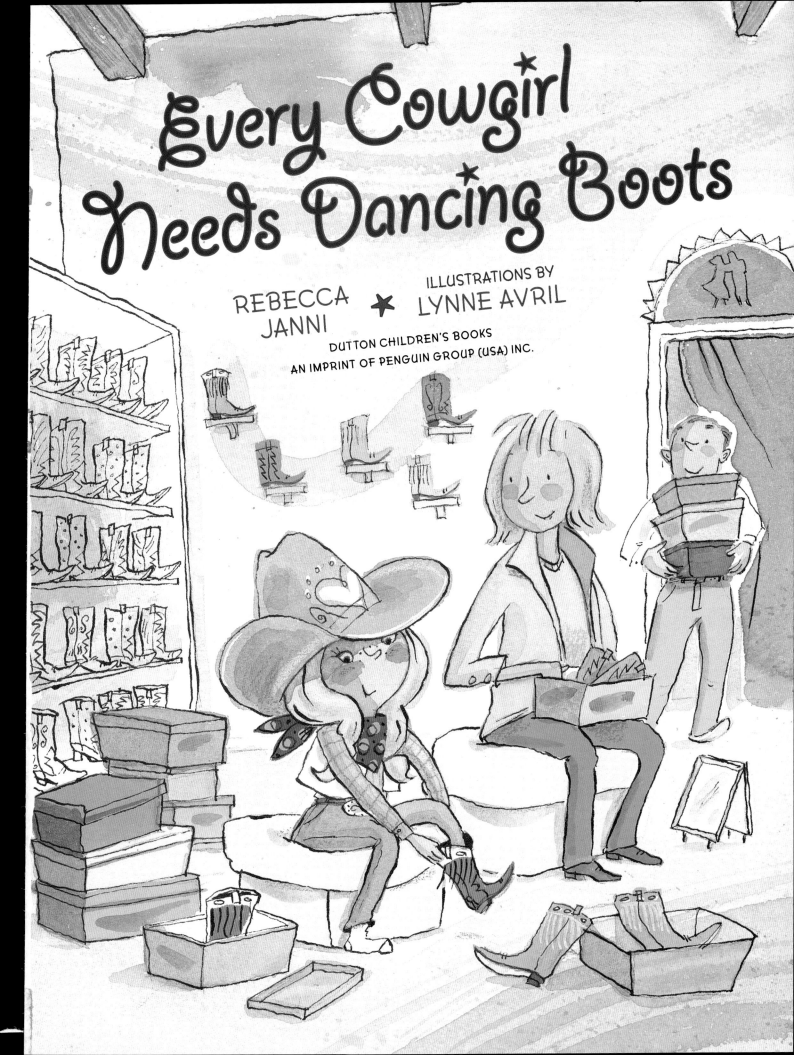

Every Cowgirl Needs Dancing Boots

REBECCA JANNI ★ ILLUSTRATIONS BY LYNNE AVRIL

DUTTON CHILDREN'S BOOKS
AN IMPRINT OF PENGUIN GROUP (USA) INC.

To Dad, who had the first dance
—R.J.

To Rosie—a cowgirl's pal through and through
—L.A.

DUTTON CHILDREN'S BOOKS • A division of Penguin Young Readers Group
Published by the Penguin Group
Penguin Group (USA) Inc., 375 Hudson Street, New York, New York 10014, U.S.A.
Penguin Group (Canada), 90 Eglinton Avenue East, Suite 700, Toronto, Ontario M4P 2Y3, Canada (a division
of Pearson Penguin Canada Inc.) • Penguin Books Ltd, 80 Strand, London WC2R 0RL, England • Penguin
Ireland, 25 St Stephen's Green, Dublin 2, Ireland (a division of Penguin Books Ltd) • Penguin Group (Australia),
250 Camberwell Road, Camberwell, Victoria 3124, Australia (a division of Pearson Australia Group Pty Ltd)
• Penguin Books India Pvt Ltd, 11 Community Centre, Panchsheel Park, New Delhi - 110 017, India • Penguin
Group (NZ), 67 Apollo Drive, Rosedale, North Shore 0632, New Zealand (a division of Pearson New Zealand
Ltd) • Penguin Books (South Africa) (Pty) Ltd, 24 Sturdee Avenue, Rosebank, Johannesburg 2196, South Africa
Penguin Books Ltd, Registered Offices: 80 Strand, London WC2R 0RL, England

Text copyright © 2011 by Rebecca Janni • Illustrations copyright © 2011 by Lynne Avril

Published in the United States by Dutton Children's Books,
a division of Penguin Young Readers Group
345 Hudson Street, New York, New York 10014
www.penguin.com/youngreaders

Designed by Irene Vandervoort • Manufactured in China • First Edition

ISBN 978-0-525-42341-6

1 3 5 7 9 10 8 6 4 2

Every cowgirl needs dancin' boots,
and I have a brand-new pair.
But you can't go dancin' all alone.

"How about making friends with those new girls across the street?" Mama said. "The youngest looks about your age."

"The glitter girls?" I asked.
I stood on tiptoes to see past the older sisters till one of 'em caught me spying. All their laughin' made me lonely. So, I did what any cowgirl would do.

I went and got my Beauty, the two-wheeled horse Mama and Daddy got me for my birthday. I put my boots in the stirrups, and we galloped out toward those glitter girls.

"Howdy there!" I hollered.
"Wanna go ridin'?"
The glitter girls shook their
heads. "Not in ballet slippers."
Hmpff, I thought. *They need
boots.*

Back home, Mama carried a tray of cookies to the table.

"I'm not hungry," I said.

But Ginger sure was. She hopped up for a closer sniff and started two-steppin' with Mama!

I laughed. "Ginger, get your dancin' boots on!
You've just given me a plan."

YOU ARE INVITED!!
1st ANNUAL
BARNYARD BASH
tonight
my house
(Nellie Sue)
LINE dancing!!
Y'ALL come!

I slung a bag over my shoulder, and Beauty and I galloped off like the Pony Express, with invites for the whole county—even the glitter girls.

"Thanks," said the youngest. "I'm Anna."

"Ballerinas don't belong in barns," said an older sister.

"There'll be popcorn and pink lemonade."

"Well, we'll think about it." She shrugged.

When Beauty and I got home, my braids were droopin' and my boots were draggin'.
"Ballerinas don't belong in barns," I told Mama.
I wished cowgirls could be quitters, but a cowgirl's got a code of honor ... so I got right to work.

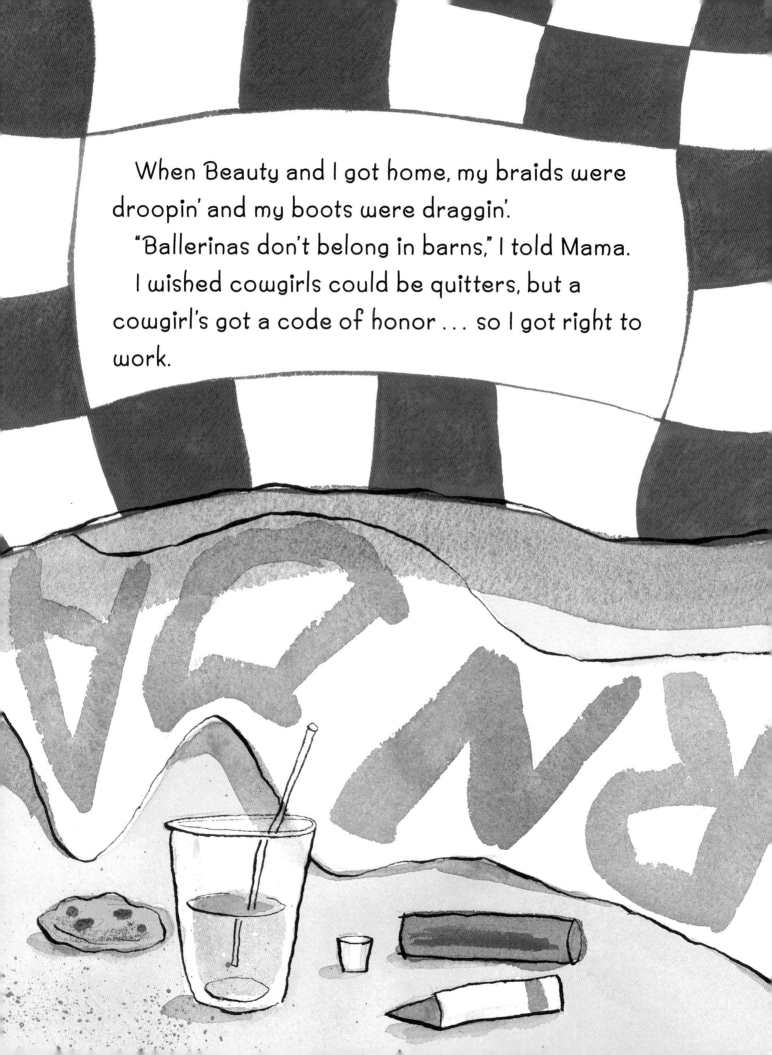

I swept the floor and scooted hay bales.

I hung lanterns from the ceiling and streamers from the rafters.

Then I hauled in the chuck wagon.
Nice and steady—so nothing spilled.

I stepped into my new boots while Mama
prettied up my braids, and I . . .

... waited

... and waited

and waited.

"Hey, Cowgirl. How about giving your first dance to Dad?"

He hoisted me up and spun me around.

When I looked over his shoulder,
I nearly lost my spurs.

The whole neighborhood was standin' by my hitchin' post! Even Anna and her glitter sisters!

I gave them a hearty cowgirl welcome, tutus and all.

When Daddy turned up the music, my dancin' boots were ready for some two-steppin'. With their slippery soles, they were perfect for scootin' along the smooth floor—nice and slick.

Maybe a little too slick. Two steps was all it took to glide into the chuck wagon and send it rollin'. The pitcher tipped, and a river of lemonade ran through the middle of my party. I slipped on a wet spot . . .

. . . and fell into the crowd.
One dancer toppled into another, and

Trip.
Slip.
Slide.

All the glitter girls went tumblin' down.

Ginger hustled over to help. She speckled the girls' leotards with paw prints and gave them sloppy kisses.

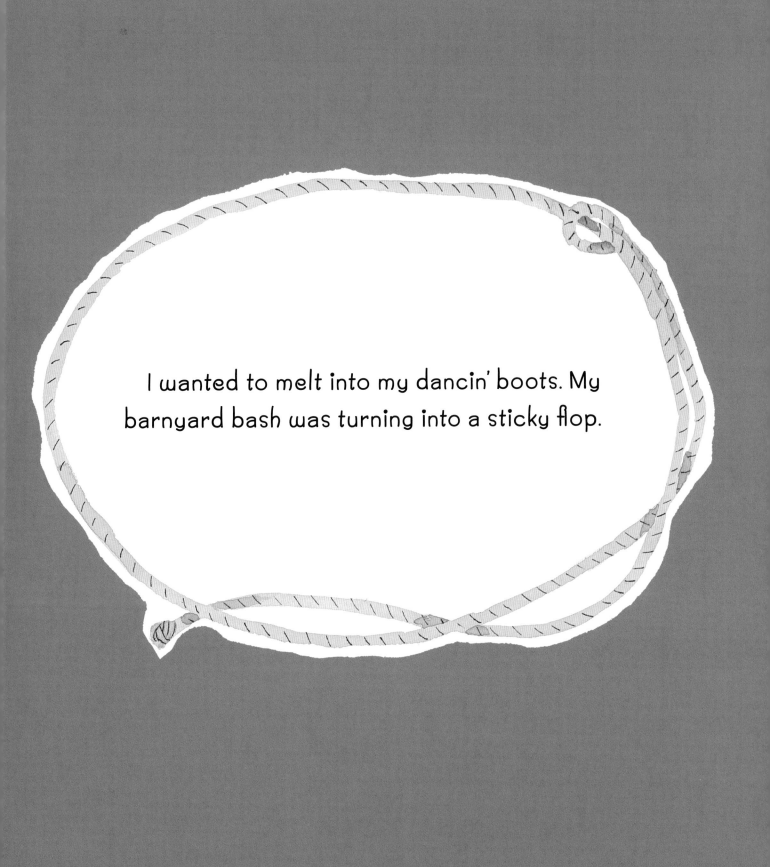

I wanted to melt into my dancin' boots. My barnyard bash was turning into a sticky flop.

But then Anna started laughing. "Pink polka dots!" she yelled. "My favorite!"

Soon everyone was laughing, and Ginger jumped and twirled even more. I gave them a bashful grin. "Look, Ginger wants to be a ballerina, too!"

"I'd rather be a cowgirl," said Anna.
I knew what I had to do—I handed over my
brand-new boots, and we lined up for our hoedown.

Because even more than dancin' boots, every cowgirl needs a friend . . .

...and I do have that.